This book belongs to

There's a Hole in my Bucket

Sung by
The Topp Twins

Pictures by
Jenny Cooper

SCHOLASTIC
AUCKLAND SYDNEY NEW YORK LONDON TORONTO
MEXICO CITY NEW DELHI HONG KONG

First published in 2011 by Scholastic New Zealand Limited
Private Bag 94407, Botany, Auckland 2163, New Zealand

Scholastic Australia Pty Limited
PO Box 579, Gosford, NSW 2250, Australia

Musical Recording and Arrangement © The Topp Twins Ltd, 2011
Illustrations © Jenny Cooper, 2011

ISBN 978-1-77543-046-9

National Library of New Zealand Cataloguing-in-Publication Data

-----

There's a hole in my bucket / music by the Topp Twins ; illustrated
by Jenny Cooper.
ISBN 978-1-77543-046-9
1. Children's songs—Texts. [1. Pails—Songs and music. 2. Songs.]
I. Cooper, Jenny, 1961- II. Topp Twins (Musical group) III. Title.
782.42083—dc 22

-----

12 11 10 9 8 7 6 5 4 3 2 1   1 2 3 4 5 6 7 8 9 / 1

Illustrations created in 2B pencil, watercolour paint and some acrylic paint.

Publishing team: Diana Murray, Penny Scown and Annette Bisman
Designed by Book Design Ltd www.bookdesign.co.nz
Typeset in Liam 30/36pt by Book Design Ltd
Printed in China by RR Donnelley

Scholastic New Zealand's policy, in association with RR Donnelley, is to use papers that are
renewable and made efficiently from wood grown in sustainable forests, so as to minimise its
environmental footprint.

There's a **hole** in my bucket,
dear Liza, dear Liza,

There's a **hole** in my bucket,
dear Liza,
   a hole.

Then fix it, dear Henry, dear Henry, dear Henry,
Then fix it, dear Henry, dear Henry,
fix it!

With what shall I fix it, dear Liza, dear Liza?
With what shall I fix it, dear Liza,

with what?

With a straw, dear Henry, dear Henry, dear Henry,
With a straw, dear Henry,
dear Henry,
a straw.

The straw is too long, dear Liza, dear Liza,
The straw is too long, dear Liza,
too long.

Then cut it, dear Henry, dear Henry, dear Henry,
Then cut it, dear Henry,
dear Henry,
cut it.

With what shall I cut it,

dear Liza, dear Liza?

With what shall I cut it, dear Liza,
with what?

With an axe, dear Henry, dear Henry, dear Henry,
With an axe, dear Henry, dear Henry,

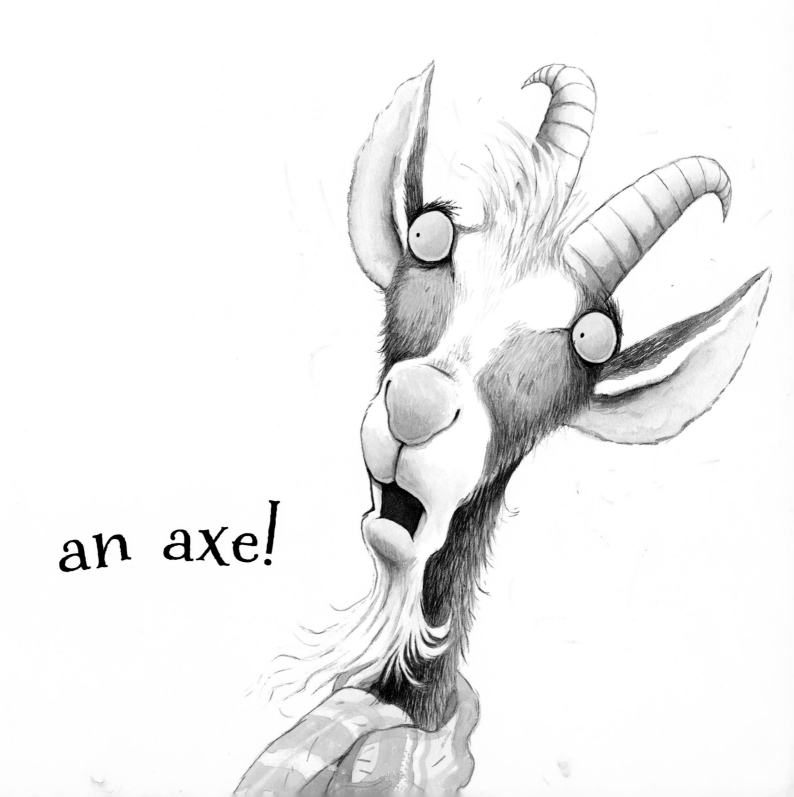

an axe!

The axe is too dull, dear Liza, dear Liza,
The axe is too dull, dear Liza,
too dull.

Then sharpen it, dear Henry, dear Henry, dear Henry,
Then sharpen it, dear Henry, dear Henry, sharpen it.

With what shall I sharpen it, dear Liza, dear Liza?
With what shall I sharpen it, dear Liza,

with what?

With a stone, dear Henry, dear Henry,
dear Henry,

With a stone, dear Henry,
dear Henry,

a stone.

The stone is too dry, dear Liza, dear Liza,
The stone is too dry, dear Liza,
too dry.

Then wet it, dear Henry,
dear Henry, dear Henry,
Then wet it, dear Henry,
dear Henry,
wet it.

With what shall I wet it, dear Liza, dear Liza?
With what shall I wet it, dear Liza,

with what?

With water, dear Henry, dear Henry, dear Henry,
With water, dear Henry, dear Henry,
with water!

In what shall I carry it, dear Liza, dear Liza?
In what shall I carry it, dear Liza,
in what?

In a **bucket**, dear Henry, dear Henry, dear Henry,
In a **bucket**, dear Henry, dear Henry,
a **bucket**.

But...
there's a hole in my bucket,
dear Liza,
dear Liza,

There's a hole in my bucket, dear Liza,

a hole!

About the Topp Twins

The Topp Twins are a truly original comic and musical duo that can undoubtedly be called a cultural institution. Their unique blend of seriously good original country music, comedy characters and some of the finest yodelling you'll hear anywhere has won them many awards and accolades. Most recently, their feature documentary film **The Topp Twins, Untouchable Girls** has screened and won awards in cinemas around the world.

From rural backwaters to hugely successful tours in New Zealand, Australia, Canada, the USA and Britain, as well as award-winning comedy television, the Topp Twins' appeal is infectious.

They see **There's a Hole in My Bucket** as a fun way to encourage kids to pick up a book, believing that learning to read is vital, no matter who you are or where you are from.

About Jenny

From the outside, I look like someone sitting at a desk twiddling a pencil and staring at a wall. But inside my head is a very busy place, full of dancing goats, short-tempered ducks and other nonsense.

Sometimes my pencil behaves and sometimes it doesn't. Since I love drawing goats and ducks and all things dancing, my pencil behaved very well for this book. Because of the hairiness of the goat, most of the book was painted using a tiny brush with only 6 hairs. By the end, the brush looked like this:

For my next book, I am going to paint something shiny, with no hair at all. Maybe a fish.

As I drew, I listened to the song — over 200 times. And even after all those times, the bucket still didn't get fixed! In case you are wondering … in the olden days (when your dad was a boy), there was no electricity and people would sharpen an axe by running it over a wet stone. A wooden bucket with a hole could be fixed by having a twig or splinter of wood hammered into the hole, and trimmed off at each end with a sharp axe. That was back in the day before shops had been invented. (Ask your mum, she will remember.)